mouthmark ,

Thirteen Fairy Negro Tales

literary pointillism on a funked-out canvas

Thirteen Fairy Negro Tales

mouthmark series
Printed and Bound in the United Kingdom

Published by mouthmark, 2005
www.flippedeye.net/mouthmark
the pamphlet series of flipped eye publishing
All Rights Reserved

First Edition
Copyright © Inua Ellams 2005

Cover Design by Inua Ellams, phaze05.com
Series Design © flipped eye publishing, 2005

ISBN: 1-905233-04-3

Thirteen Fairy Negro Tales

This is dedicated
to capsules of walking water
– sculpted by the wind.

Inua Ellams
2005

mouthmark *poetry is a kind of literary pointillism applied on a jazz-blues-blood-sex-rock-and-rolled canvas with sweat, tears and spittle as primary colours; if you don't get it you're not listening...*

Contents

Thirteen Fairy Negro Tales

Thirteen Fairy Negro Tales 7

Gangsters, Geishas and Goat herdsmen...11

Mono Moveism..14

Midnight Music Marauders.. 17

Royal Displacement 20

The Last Rebels...23

Babylon Battle Babble 26

Alice in Never-Lover Land 29

The One About God...33

Brother's Keeper Person Thing 36

The Last Bohemian..39

Dustbin Diaries.. 41

Swahilian Gingerbread Men..44

I spun 13 fairy Negro tales that night.
Weighed them on illogic scales
that tipped the balance
and formed an alliance
with my version of the truth,
I uprooted reality and substituted it
for another that had more humanity;
thinking that if I thought hard enough
I'd make it real.

Having so much belief in mind power
I cowered beneath the defunct light
and attempted to bend Saturn's rings
around my mind.
I did this till the blinds let light in
to wake me from that super sonic slumber.
I swore I was under the influence of lightening
that struck my brain and convinced me I could stain worlds at a time.

But I realized it was just beer and wine.

I found I could dine on the sun
drink the milky- way
let stars stick to my tongue
clasp Orion around my waist
pluck Pluto, paste him to Mars and run
before Zeus realized I had face-lifted his estate.

I found I could reverse 360
from the 3 point line
and dunk Jupiter in a black hole.
But this divine world existed
only in my soul.

So I held my 13 Negro tales
and made a back bone
swapped it for my own
stood to the wind and dared earth
to spin me off it shoulders
not knowing I had soldered my pen to its core
and "ink"-planted a metaphor.

And perhaps this was just in my mind,
but I'd envisioned my self as a poet, so let it be
'cause I write this not for you,
just for me.
I'm trying to make the world a lil' better
by building bridges out of letters
trying to break the sound barrier
and obliterate the color lines,
'cause I was taught race was in the mind:
You can unwrap the illusions and unwind
to the sound of rainbow drops falling
on all proletarian props.

I speak thus
for I fell in love with an Iranian
girl who complimented my soul.
She had no color;
just a diamond backbone.
I looked in her eyes and saw five stories
for each tale I owned.
Though we never dated,
she sowed a seed in me
and I reap the fruits regularly
and mix the juice with ink,
so when I write about love
it tends to smell of her.

She is my virtue and my curse.

I guess I'm a fairy tale less now,
guess I have to chill at bus stops
and smoke sess now,
guess I have to trail blaze
and be like "yes now"
to every soul who gazes at me
trying to guess how
I can talk to myself and care less
about the effects of stress.
It's cause Spokenword is like sex,
the more you listen,
the better it gets.

That's why on long bus rides,
I close my eyes and try to hear drumbeats
from Nigeria- the mother land calling.
I be like "yes mum, I'm hearing ya"
It's like some ciphered world
with armies of sounds
and underground cultures
with talon-less vultures
trying to pierce my skin
and place talking drums within.

But Hip Hop takes over
and my head bobs to the beats
of a different soldier
and it's gotten colder
on this side of thought
'cause now,
I hear dreams money bought.

Driven despondent by this
I close my eyes tighter and
think a little deeper.
I see aquatic worlds
ruled by Soulquarians,
gods that remix bubbles with beats
so we inhale music
swap smiles for CD's
do voodoo just for the hell of it
and there is no pressure
if you choose to be celibate.

That's another fairy tale gone.
That's another scenario
I'd offered to the Sun
to run on Monday mornings
when workers are still torn
between workdays and fun.

A world without guns
when the only people running
are kids chasing nuns
for trying to convert them
when their teeth where still gums.

But the sun shrugged his shoulders
and shoved my idea where he couldn't see.
Telling me the cosmos didn't agree,
telling me humanity needed drama
in order to be free.
So I popped my middle finger
for Martin Luther King,
Seamus Heaney and Palestine's plea,
'cause you shouldn't need to suffer
to be granted mercy,
post-depression insurrection
is not a way to be.

But this world exists
between the purple evenings
that serve as backdrops to my reasoning
and nestle hopes of seasoning the world
with constructive dope,
to raise minds to that nexus in the sky
distill the plexus and finally understand
why Tupac, Biggie and Jim Morrison had to die.

I guess I'm more fairy tales less now
guess it's best if I tell you the rest now;
like how roots are looped through violin strings
and red mists faded yellow yell:
"the last bohemian lives!"…
like how Alice never loved in Never Land
and The last Rebels rise to remix riffs…

But the last fairy story
goes a bit like this:
I sit on a mountain top
with my Iranian scented ink
trace words on winds
sink to blue worlds
drink nectar
and think…

   and
     think.

Once upon a time
in a kingdom of thought
on the death bed of parchment
along the pathways of discovery
uncovered in the blind movements
of a mind that dared to move men;

from the random scribbling
of a search for meaning and insight
a dying pen wrote revolutiona-realistically
of a secret carved into the rock face of life.

It reads of a concept,
conducive to the conquests of cohorts
conspiring to keep human hope alive.
It is divine intellect
base-lined in bridging the gaps
from gangsters and gats
to Mongolian goat herdsmen grazing
growing geishas star-gazing and
a girl with a gift in her grasp.

It reads, *We are all reflections of each other.*

I believe this to be true.

I believe that the might
of a medieval blacksmith
moulding metal in a forge
whose mystic assistance stretches
no further than a hammer's scourge
is reflected in the endless courage
of a working class mother making hot meals
in both of her dead end jobs.

I believe that the fear of a hood-rat
tasked with stealing five cars; that pressure
that doubt, that pause…
is found in a ballet dancer with already red toes
asked to pirouette through five bars.

I know that when a drunk hits rock bottom
when light sears through the undergrowth
of his reality and he sees truth
that moment of sudden clarity
is mirrored in the seconds a scientist spies
the last lines of a mathematical thesis
and turns it into truth.

I know that once
in the courtyards of colour
a glimmer from the fortress of thought came forth
bearing notions of using pure hues on canvas.
That was the birth of Impressionism.
A reflection of that movement
moved MCs to remix their mental motions
and that was the birth of Hip Hop's keeping it realism.

And Behold!
On the balconies of the Age of Aquarius
it shall be told
that of the many soldiers that have fallen
few rode bold into battle convinced
by the reasons for which they fought.
That fact is reflected in the life struggles
of every day people.

This uncertainty spawns the freethinkers,
the 'Freaks'
and the fury of the last bohemian
screaming "power to those freaks"
is a reflection of the fury
with which I write

I WRITE IN THUNDER SPEAK!

that turns lightning to mere weather
glows so my word plays
could be the earth glows that bathe
thought flows into submission.

My mission is to be the very best
that I can be. So often at street corners
I speak to locals, grab the essence
of their spirits in a choke hold and squeeze
till their truth emits from my vocals;
so I can walk the waking
woe calls of we
and find a new me
in the voices of others.

So if by the end of this
you don't believe in a reflection
of yourself, just trust
that your soul has been lathered
across the cusps of mirrors world wide
and within him, her or me,
you can find an image of yourself.
Because collectively
we reflect infinity amongst
ourselves, living
happily
ever
after.

Thousands of feet from the death
place of Icarus, miles from wilting
wet wax wings and water crystals freezing
to nothingness; of the tribe of Israel, lying
between the lands of Judah and Azekah
weather beaten into rank, flanked on both sides
by faceless rebel rubies

there is a pebble
that remembers Goliath
there is a sling that remembers victory
there is a song that remembers joy.

Under sharp stones and bare feet
under dusty courtyards and half buried secrets;
five steps from misplaced identities
and misled theories
two miles from dry prayer mats
and interstellar symbols called into life
by a Muslim man, mauling the wind
with soul-bred callings to prayer
peppered by bullet-shaped words
and wicked agendas on weary nights;
wrought of wood, buried six feet under
loose gravel and broken pillars of hate

there is an empty plate
that remembers Ghandi,
there is a linen cloth
that remembers death.

In the citadels of ancient Greece
past the stone monuments to myths and legends
that guard the gateways to gods and goddesses
past perforated pillars and perennial peeling
frescoes that flake;
behind that, behind the fountains that flicked water
on sweat-wetted marble;
in the corner ruins of a bath house
bathed in unbroken peace
unscathed and partially scripted

there is parchment
that remembers Plato,
there is a pen
that remembers thought.

And through that, look.
Look to the last century, from Georgia's red hills
to the mole hills of Mississippi, from the mountains
of New York, to the peaks of California, look.
From the snow capped Rockies of Colorado
to the deserts of Texas, look.
Through race riots, flaming crosses
and chain gangs clad in white, through night
through prayers whispered from bruised lips
through knees bent, lips locked
through sentences to death
and besetting breath, look.
Through empty seats at the backs of buses
and bent resurrections of hope, through courage
eloping with strength, through lengthy winters
and withered minds through conviction unwinding
to a backdrop of bedraggled Bibles
covered in blood,
　　"though weeping may endure for a night,
　　joy comes with the morning"
so look through it.
Look to the coming of the Sun
and spirits soaring through sound
look through a million men marching
with fists thrown up!

Married to that memory
there is a microphone
that remembers Martin Luther King
there are men that still dream.

And in the basements of moth eaten project buildings
beneath black bohemian bookshelves
and brown bathrooms, there is a backroom
baptized with sweat and tears.
Before it, an un-vacuumed space
filled with broken boom boxes,
archaic electronics and drumsticks

resting on dead drums gone humdrum
interwoven with expired wires and quiet
speaker boxes that peak through the shadows.
Caught amongst this current of silent
symphonies of rare riffs and rivers of rough
rhythms, rounded with dust

there is a fractured needle
that first free styled funk
there is broken vinyl that remembers flesh
there is a deck that remembers Grand Master Flash...

These men are testaments to the notion
that one man can make a movement
one child can start the change
so as this poem reaches its range
believe that beneath your clothes beats
a heart that beats to the backdrop of destiny
believe that you possess the power
you are the form of suns, believe that
your actions can cause a reaction that snowballs
into an avalanche of word wide will
and by your movements
someday, we may reach that zenith
of happily, ever, and after.

If music be the food of love, play on.

And we played on that night.
Like a mellow cello player, high
on milk and melanin, making
bone marrow music, we played
like a sparrow musing on Beethoven
using the borrowed wings of wordless
words, absorbing Gaia through fingers
probing, blunt swords through soft butter.

We played like a guitar riff
uttered from Venus, shuddered
from the rocking shoulders of a colour
blind pianist, like a stream of beauty
seam-less, we played like the seamstress
of sound sewing soul-quaric pulses
in the lands of eardrums, drawing treble clefs
on brown cliffs, clawing at soaring notes
daring them to lift our spirits.

We played like a dead French kiss reincarnated
as a saxophone with tendencies to hiss
galaxophonic secrets through the tombs of trombones
reborn as the lower bones of Bojangles, dancing
on base drums prancing like songs of the railroad
set free, we played like freedom, stirring
on those hills reflected in the back heels
of a dancer in New Orleans
tapping prosperity

on concrete;
we played like the rose that grew
from concrete.

With its roots looped in violin strings
strung through harmonicas, planted in the wind
whistling tales of smelling just as sweet
weeping wet willows of wonder through pillows
producing sounds that slunk silently into darkness
we played like the Moonlight.

We were The Music.
We Danced.
Like two zephyrs with a license to live
later lolling like two lullabies, childlike
and moronic, stereophonic, hydrophonic
like a tonic squeezed from xylophones fed
to a young horn blower, blowing harmonious
tones of one to a cloud communion
resulting in a light rusty rain…

We played like rain-dust falling
dusting backstreets and high rise
buildings with homeopathic water
causing memories of Marvin Gaye, Jackson Five
Sam Cooke, The Supremes, Steve Wonder;
and we left that. We left the old memories
of Motown and came to the happenings of now
became two turntables spinning infinity
using incense sticks as needles
scratching divinity from vinyl, revealing
a soft state of existence we never knew existed.

   Like being caged in a marshmallow
   being tied with smoke
   being Saturn's sun-stroked
   being lathered by a rose

We became of the fellows with no sense
of reality- I became the base drum
and she became that rhythm, adlibbing
free-flowing, free-styling, mad-living
like a symphony growing through hoops
entwining with its bass beginning roots.

That night, we played like a quartet
of dare devils drunk on Jasmine Juice
pulse- racing, temperature- rising
heartbeats audio-basing
in a big brilliant bang of blue
music, like a bison billowing through fog

And by the dying light, we parted with a hug
leaving the ghosts of galaxies

to congregate around our echoes
and create new worlds
from our laughter patterns
and live happily
ever
after.

Once upon a time
in a Kingdom far away
there lived a queen
with star maps in her palms.

She walked as one born in the third creek
from which the Nile eventually crept
she aired the essence of calm
capped in pupils as deep as psalms
from which she drew the secrets of life
and placed them in spoken shadows
for generations to reap and swallow
till wisdom wallowed
in the centres of their thought.

She had but to breathe out of beat
and sons darker than blue
would surround her in her sleep,
guard her till she stirred back to life
having deciphered theories
buried in the fields of her dreams
drawn from that Kingdom's conscience.

And I speak of no Kingdom in fiction.
I speak of one whose strength was sold
when gold aired its valediction.
I speak of one whose own rendition of all
called souls to come fall by its edition
and fold their cold theories written in folly.

I speak of the old kingdom of Mali

where unturned stones held in their grasps
fables that lapsed back to the start of time
fables, ladled and passed back on specific
breathing patterns, spoken to the lights
of flared lanterns on cold nights
gaining relevance in vocal flight
till entire villages were taught to recite
the metaphoric histories of ethics and life.

I speak of Mali
where stars rallied at night time

moon blue
scattering the heavens with pin pricks of light
through which like minds flew and listened
to the teachings of elders
banned from all labour.

Back there,
she had fortune's favour
now she is simply the next door neighbour.

Displaced, this Queen slaves under starless skies
in high-rise buildings and office blocks pushing
broomsticks and mops through cubicles for a living.
To ease the pain in her tired back
she packs her senses behind stacks
of sun filled memories and hums
distilled work songs
grilled under Malian suns
to match the sweep of her arm's swing.

You've seen her;
that aging woman who sings
in a strange and raspy voice
songs that have caused
the unused parts of me to gasp
and rejoice in the simple pleasure
of being alive.
Her songs are sonic hives of pain
that force me to close both eyes
and taste the bitter juice of beaten joys
slain by famine, plague and pestilence.
In the vague silence from which
    her songs reach me,
they breach the brick walls of my being;
slam like psalms through the red rocks
of my mental blocks
freeing my senses
from the false defences
of thinking that this lady is that
little bit crazy.

With my eyes closed
I start to listen
breath turns cold
reality goes that little bit hazy

and I find myself in the backwaters
of her history, painting pictures
with the perfect palette
of her words.

And she sings
of waking up one starless night
finding her household struck by a plague
bodies lying cold un-speckled un-aged;
of an unborn child caged in its dead mother's womb
desperately kicking for breath
destined for death
and not even having lived yet;
of cradling her last grandchild
giving all she had
just to reach the next morning
and find herself yawning
on a stiffened face
eyes still open, pointed to the stars
no pulse, no pace, as his soul soars
and she is left, locked behind the bars
of living, all alone;

of finally leaving her home, to a distant land
where elders are murdered for gold and money
and even in the summer
the sun shines cold.

But she lives on
bruised and bold
singing her sweet songs
so the masses hear them.

As she walks that famished road
a single thought guides her;

that when she dies
her spirit will gain that
ultimate prize and she
will live that
happily ever
after-life.

In a galaxy far, far away;
in the cradle clutch of destiny
in the arms of fate, in the bottomless
bowls of eventuality,
the beat goes on.

Through the blocked ears of walls
that have learnt not to listen
and the partings of lips
that have learnt to tell tall tales
in bare basements and brown bathrooms
the rhythm is ceaseless and no matter
how much we deny the truth
the beat goes on
and on.

The last rebels
watch the sun go down.
They watch the silent silhouettes
flint- headed censor the spotlight.
Now forced to navigate with only thought
they buy through the false theories
and re-master the muffled memories
of a time mime free.
They dine
on seasoned remnants
of history wishing to resurrect them;
but there are setbacks.

From that Galaxy,
the last rebels look
to the second continent
and see the contortion of truth
where the sick are led to believe
that raping babies
is an AIDS relief.

From that galaxy,
the last rebels look
to the western hemisphere
and witness the folly of men

where thirteen feet
from a full food disposal system
lies a half-conscious kid
who has to rest
after 13 steps
cause his body
running on empty
can't abide that stress
and he sends his sprit to syringe the stars
lest, driven hopeless
he submits to death
via collision and cars.

And worse still
the last rebels watch
as, under the guise of "epidemics"
the powers that be test out viruses
on many proletarians.
Of that many
the humanitarian few
who know the truth are silenced
so the secrets lie hidden
within rhythm of life
and the last rebels sit
knives at the ready
and watch the beat
go on.

Now what if I were to tell you
that we are The Last Rebels;

that in this galaxy it has been said
that a man-powered plague plagued recently
and we called it SARS;

would you Rise up?
Would you Riot?
Would you Rage?

Would that even make a change?
I think not.

Because at the heart of the human problem
is the problem of the human heart.

To cause these conflicts to depart
our part is to remix the rhymes that rhyme within
flip that beat and dance to a new theme;
one that doesn't falsify or cover up
causing men to die
causing men to commit suicide;
one without police brutality
bursting at the edges...
and yes

I believe in the existence of police brutality.
The fatalities of men, darker than blue
have danced through the vapours of my inkwells
have lanced through the shells of truth
their magnified absences are the fruits
and till we feed
we shall ever go hungry.

So the beat goes on
cross galaxy
the beat goes on
never knowing ever strong
the beat goes on
all knowing, all wrong
the beat goes on
the beat goes on
the beat goes on.

Once upon a time
In a kingdom far, far away
it was thought that the fathers of fortune
feathered the wings of beggars and bettered
the winds of change.

It was thought that fate smiled
on those who toiled while the sun shined;
thought, that the luminary minds of men
could make the mountain range
strange to its own peak.

I speak of worlds where metaphors
were the building blocks of teachings
the sonic backdrop of songs were further reaching;
not a mis-educated, mis-vocalist's preaching
about her future husband's wallet
breaching the realms of normality
before love could reach informality.

I speak of worlds where
wars were last resorts visited in scenarios evident.
Now, bombs drop through thoughts flawed
mind power rendered irrelevant.
Distant nebulae that once nestled
in the bellies of thought streams
have been forced to stay unseen
as time stretches on.

I speak of worlds
that once spawned rock solid morals
instead of all being pawned for the dollar
and 50 Cents. Mass spasms of spondulick interference
send men claiming to be *dogs* and *cats*, path-strayed.
Because the path back to God lies
in the realization that we are just
human.

And this world is jungle.

We stand in the centre, fuming
led by snakes into the maze of thorns
thickets and Bush-es.

The time will come when we stand
beneath the solar plexus of the sun
and demand to be free
mine are the lost soliloquies of redemption songs
I hope you will stand and sing with me.

I hope you will sing
when I speak of worlds
where pro-optic stardust
layered all pupils and all souls could star
the sky, dance like metaphysical butterflies
tracing happy trails through the third age
of a global lie, exhuming the true meaning of life.

And I speak of worlds
where fathers fathered
the notion that all females flowered as queens
and from their fountains
kings would rise
planting feathers
in the shadows of their footsteps.

Mothers mothered the notion that
other than love, nothing mattered.
But paper chasing atoms have scattered
that pattern of thought, Nike's bought
the revolution, we charge through life
dodging boulders of mass confusion
like: "don't think, *Just do it*",

but mine is the chosen path through chaos;
I'll run through it.

I search for higher learning.
I am yearning to move on
but we are living in Babylon.
So I search for *Spokenword* spots
to open mike and babble on
about being here, trying
to vocally express the fears
locked in the spineless tears
of symphonies of silent souls.
These often exist
in the abyss of my own
so I battle on

trying to save myself –
once whole

I have been scattered and pattered
among the fields of everyday people
our destinies are tied together
for better or worse
I pose and prose and speak word.

And if the day comes
that these forces grow
greater than my might
I will not go gently into that good night
I will stay and fight.
Forced to the navy corners of isolation
I will ignore the call of desperation
fall to my knees and take my last breath
wielding my vocal sword's echo
till death
WORD

word
word
word
word
word
…
..
.

Once upon a time
in a kingdom far away
in the thirteenth hour of night
eleven lightings after dreams come out to play
nine seconds from a kiss goodnight
for the seventh time, a little girl sits
on a floor cross-legged
flips open a book titled
"13 Fairy Negro Tales"
finds her page in five seconds
and in three moments
and two blinks
focuses on a description
of one brown woman…

"In a mountain made entirely of soil
a blue crystal was grown
and its seeds were thrown
to the sands from which oceans
and seas came forth.
"This woman's hands
were moulded by the farmer
who toiled that mountain's land.

"Her bones were crafted from Ivory
sold to the artists of the Titans
who were told to create with it
something greater than themselves.
They kept those bones
shelved them till they were
reincarnated as light
and baptised them in the unseen hues
of rainbows which solidified and became
whole, so when she moved
her shadows echoed spectrums.

"Her shoulder blades once waded in Maya
and emerged making moon ripples
on the Mesolithic rock face of ever.

*"Like the ghosts of lilies
flock printed on slate
her cheeks skin-kiss
the gates of a brown heaven.
Her voice is rooted in the fantastic
flying like silk
fed on feather fractals
falling like angel zest."*

And I know that woman.
We have conversed.

Many times,
I have cycled through the cities
of her psyche and left graffiti growing
on the walls her mental
making music
using palms as amplifiers
losing myself in the masts
of a friendship made to last.
And when I realised that this
between us, this might be
the stuff of greatness
I stopped.

Took a step back

tore my heart off my sleeve
and offered it to her
on a silver platter saying:
  "Lady
take this.
Wipe your soul with it.
Wear it when the winds change.
Sew it into a cushion and sleep on it
beneath the changing boughs
of the woes of the world
wear me like a breast plate
keep me like a glove, lady
let me Love you."

But she said "No,
it's far too late".

She said that in the past
she had been disappointed, failed;
that men that are not smart;
men with flawed logic
and lazy feet
climbed through the windows of her soul
to the bowels of her belly
and left seeds of weeds
that be eternally growing
eternally towing
eternally tugging
at the small saplings of beauty
left in her heart, and *she would not*
she could not start nothing with no one;
there was no place for love
none.

None.

And that
    left me lost …
  in the winter
of her solitude
caught in a courtyard
of dying roses and
dead crystals
with one pen to coat me
from the cold.

One pen.

So with that pen
I am painting a new portrait.

It is of a man, who sculpts crystals for a living
whose pupils are calibrated
to reflect that woman's own
whose hugs mimic Maya
who is wiling to be the earth for her to grow on
and be cherished; a man to replenish.

And when this portrait is finished
when it is nailed to parchment

I shall mail it to the mystics
hoping that they cast it into living
hoping that fate comes around to my way
of seeing and makes him be
so he can live *her* for me
so he can love her
for me
for that is what poets do

we dream.

we dream
in the thirteenth hour of night
eleven lightings after playtime
nine seconds before a kiss goodnight,
before a little girl closes a book of tales...

leans back to sleep, leaving a *bag lady* locked
in the pages of an experience;
me half empty; both
subconsciously wishing for

happily
ever
after.

In a galaxy far, far away
in the grand canyons
of an afro-hued wilderness
before the naturally formed
symbol of fertility; raised from rock
born of wind and wisdom, locked
to the uncontrolled, uncorked
gateway to all worlds and all words;
to the left of a camp fire fuelled
by wooden swords; sits a purple man
with sky blue pupils and sand dusted hands.

In his left hand, he holds 3.6 cowry shells
2 pens, one scroll times infinity.
In his right, he holds a mic, which he raises
to his lips, turns to face the north and speaks:

"I have seen God! "
"Last week, he walked like Osirus.
He was last seen selling incense sticks
to girls on street corners. The day before
he sat mourning his bullet battered friend -
another black man turned to dust.
Despite the heartache and the rust
the next day, with his emotions
nailed to his sleeve and his spirit lost
he was back at that street corner
barely standing on his feet
still selling".

Saying this, old man turns
to the eastern world and whispers:

"I have seen God,
at the tender age of six,
kidnapped from his family,
assigned a bed of bricks, 3 bullets,
one gun and five rebel songs, he was
bullied into battle and forced to partake
in random scores of killing.
As fortune would have it, he was captured

dropped on a landmine and left lower limb-less
yet in anti war rallies
you can hear his voice
preaching peace".

Saying this he turns
to the south and says to the southern wind:

"I have seen God.
She walks with death.
She was informed she had terminal
cancer and a few months to live. Today
5 years late, she runs marathons to raise funds
to research and combat that cancerous killing.
In spite of that ever tightening
noose towards her last hour
she refuses to cower with fright;
she stands and fights".

And with the wind speed rising
shadows and silhouettes flying
to welcome the night, this purple
man turns to the western word and bellows to the dying light;

"I HAVE SEEN GOD!
she was disguised as Shawana
a single mother. She rocks two jobs
three kids, two cars and gives change to homeless
others. She can go from corporate to ghetto
she rocks red stilettos with earth brown badus
and has cowry shells laced
to her laptop carry-case."

With that, he vanished into nothingness
but his last blue breath said this:

"We spend so much time looking to heaven
that we put ourselves through hell.
We ignore the daily miracles that line our streets
looking for supernatural signs that God exists
when it is written: *God exists within us*

This is found everywhere:
in the diaries of Shamen. Found
in the log books of logarithms
doodled on the petals of each rose
that grows from rock; it is hidden
in the souls of sell-outs
sprinkled on the sands
of time; it is stamped
on the palms of check-out girls
paying their way through college
and 90 year old dreads
still seeking knowledge;
it is paraphrased from Biblic verses
versed in Quranic lines;
it is found in rap
rhythm and rhyme
it is bared on the conquered
mountain of Everest
it is now left for y'all to take,
rest and be as
happily, ever, after
as you can.

Once upon a time,
there lived a man.
Born to the speech patterns
of street slang, he was raised
to the ever present sounds of sirens
wailing through the effervescent
failing lights of a brick-city estate

Fatherless from birth
he modelled himself on thugs
stole and dealt drugs, then caught
and convicted, he was locked
in lone confinement.

In the silence that followed
he saw himself- whole.
The desolation seen
sowed a new him.
So, released, he went straight
and fortune reads:
he reaped the fruits of seeds sewn pure.
But beyond the shores
of this paradise clouds loomed.

His colleagues hated the thought
of *the great unwashed* rising
through suds, clean and glistening
so they bowed their heads together
eyebrows furrowed, nostrils flared
nose hairs bristling
and plotted the fall of a man
who gave his all.

And in this same kingdom
there lived a woman.
Made to leave school
at sweet sixteen
she was forced-married to a fool
who raped her every night
till her self confidence and might
were crucified to the sounds
of her tears.

Her fears took flight
when she found a new soul
growing inside her
but her husband hit harder
and left her on her own
16 years old, pregnant
dishonored, disowned.

Like this she lived
in hostels and shacks
spirit cracked
baby strapped to her back
raiding dustbins for food
addicted to smack
to mask her life's hell

and now she sells sex,
son by her side
spirit hovering beyond reach
contemplating suicide.

And these two stories, these people
do not live far and wide
they are your friend's neighbour
your sister's old boss
the silently sitting sigh-ers on a bus.
Find them
the faceless fellows
praying in whispered bellows
that their tragedies be lightened
by human touch.

So if you see that man walking
with his spirit on a crutch
or that specific sister
raving about giving up…

If you see them

tell them I have their dreams.

Tell them I have their dreams.
Tell them that they're planted in a new age

blue festering through Aquarius, a new stage.
Tell them that that I have turned the page and
inscribed with glowing white ink
their names on the pages of tomorrow.
Tell them that hope has burrowed through their lands
and laid eggs in their earth-sands and there is a new birth
beyond the bands of that dark night.
Tell them I have seen their spotlight
and it is love-shaded.
Tell them that their storms have been sedated
by the whispered words of a bellow's exhaled
echoed last breath
for nothing lasts for ever;
even fires succumb to death.

Tell them it's always darkest before
a sunburst's first zest.

Tell them to take it easy.
Tell them to rest.

Tell them to picture the pressed
warm juices of a soft stream
no haste.
Tell them to savour those seconds.
Tell them to taste.
Tell them fortune comes to those who wait.
I have heard their futures,
their laughter rings true.
Tell them their skies are blue.
Tell them they lived
happily ever after.

Tell them that it's true.

The Last Bohemian

In a galaxy far away,
adjacent to burnt sienna sunrises and Starbucks
symbols that hover just over
forbidden land.

Hidden
behind the buildings forged
to cage thought;
echoing images of freedom un-bought
to a background of melanin music;
wrought of men that be telling what truth is,
overlooking stacks of de-framed
photographs of ol' Blue Eyes
singing *I did it my way*;
on a cliff
graffitied with colours
once imprisoned in a prism;
risen from earth and *don't-be-different* dissing;
caught in a cloud of conformity is the
dwelling place of the last bohemian.

It is a heaven for all things 'one',
a five leaf clover, a purple sun
a peeling diamond, a bullet ridden gun
a disco ball spitting sultry songs of solitude
a tube of H2O un-passed through human body
un pushed through human flesh, a painting of a Neo-
shaman moulding ocean lingo
a potion to poster a riff's row
a feline felon's forgotten flow
the recorded bellow of a new age fellow
a red mist faded yellow
a mellow-melanin-man, a first stand
a captured moment of light glinting on chrome
a shape in static, a monochrome-matic necklace
of green olives, seeds and pollen
a falling tree in a silence's constant
a constant red line with a blue period

for only through periods of constants,
is the need for change made apparent.

And the apparent parents the change in turn.
The last bohemian embodies that all:

A feather caught in a cyclone
whirl winded into the iris of a prayer
sent from a prairie, palm-kissed into existence.
A red flare in the pacific blue
a pacifist in true danger
a water baby in a sand castle
a rhythm ranger
a birth in a manger,
the metal matter of Excalibur unmade
a firefly dazzling with shade
a linen cloth on silk,
a black eyed pea floating in milk
a Griot gloating at a broken memory chip
a weather butterfly woken to walk the walk
for they that only talked the talk
a cross hatch in a gradient
a remedy in a realm of ailments
a hot rock in heaven, a hailstone in hell
a fairy negro tale teller in the land of myths and legends
a reject, registered as reverting back to one
a blue wire in a red storm, a torn sheet showing
children of the corn, chanting
"no change, no progress"

And the last bohemian be the body of progress
for the last bohemian be the body of change
and the last bohemian bears the power of birth
for the last bohemian…
is a woman.

Men are just not metal enough.

Her daughters will dance the death of revolutions
and give birth to new ones to take their place.
They will write this story before it is too late
they will live
happily
ever
after

Once
upon a time,
a young man gleaned
from an archaic continent creamed
in the light fantastic;
from the borders of history baked
before an African sun
came to this kingdom
of Babylon.

This kingdom became his home.
And as time turned its page
suit followed his age –
this now withered warrior
is whom I see before me.

The way his sits shows
that his toes were once kissed
by born again rain dancers.
You can read the wisdom
in his posture, you can taste it.
With his back straight
face forward, shoulders broad
you can tell that he was made to lord over many;
you can sense the toasts of the past, those-loyal-to-life
casting coats his way.
The dustbin he sits on wears
the ghost formation of a throne cast in light
shown only if you squint with your third eye
and let ether-light loan itself to the moment.

History is grooved in his garments.
The heaviness drags his movements
as chains clink on his collar.
The Mississippi that burns on his right shoulder
is dowsed with the water ways
of Saro Wiwa on his left.
The pride of escaped slaves rises from them
like the steam created when magma hits seawater.
The zest of greatness rests on his chest
gracing all that is he, intoxicating all that is me

culminating in his presence growing, dignity glowing
seven inches past his torn and tattered clothes.

But in the wake of all this glory,
I sense his light dimming towards its close.

So I wish.
I wish for a star studded tobacco leaf
filled with newly made mortal matter
meaning for him to smoke it
and defer the coming of the last latter
so he may live longer
but all that I reap is the wind.

Instead
I reach into my pocket
and retract a handful of me
disguised as silver coins
and drop it into the empty coffee cup
beside him "Sir", I whisper, foolishly
trying to use those coins as payment
to the pastures of his spirit. "Sir", I say
once again, expecting to gain entrance
to the campsites of his soul, "Sir, Old
man, how did it get to be like this?"

Silence.

In the empty seconds that follow
He is still. Like a gathering of mango
farmers awaiting the moon rise
or children, breaths held
awaiting the Griot's first message
like a choir of pencils
waiting to chorus words
or wash women of the Nile
awaiting Cleopatra's descent
He is still.

Then he stirs.

He stirs like a mountain
streaked with silver dread locks

like a black tide coming in
commanding time to witness
one of its many prodigal sons
he stares and says...

"Son,
the world just ain't big enough no more.
We have devalued the mystery of life
for the values of materialistic living
I am from a time when whole villages mourned
our passing, and now the masses complain
that we live too long.

Son, I am past my die-by date.
These silver pieces of your soul means
that I shall marvel at the moon once more
but it is far too late, move on son
you can do no more.
Just take with you this truth,
we are the *'yous'* of yesterday.
You will become the *'wes'* of tomorrow.
If you do not wish to live on a trash can like this
then you must walk in our shoes today."

The silence after he speaks
is stone aged.

I walk gently into the night,
thankful to have been kissed
with a vital catalyst
for living happily
ever
after.

A long ago time in this kingdom
key holes were more than gateways
granting entrance to the other side.

Pebbles were much more
than rebel ambassadors of a rock
face and the powers that letters wore
yielded much more than messages.

Around each square moment of existence
mysteries were littered like lilies in snow.
Since then
the winters have grown wilder
but those white whispers are still
peeking through the snow
and if you haven't seen them
yet, someday you will see them too.

In the cracks of pavements
you will see them;

Armies of Swahilian gingerbread men
sipping opium water
and lemon drops
licking the last cranberry crystal crops
off the backs of blue lady bugs
begging them to once again dictate
the story of ever.

You will hear them
choirs of Celtic b-boys
rocking Scottish kilts
creating soft-rock-reggae
in an old railway station
radiating reason to recess
with their voices receding down hallways
and their echoes returning
always
always
always....

You will smell them
the fragrance of forgotten forefathers

and the faded fractals of fauna found
on the windowsills to wisdom
and in the spines of books.

You will see them
serenaded in sunrise
testimonials of young time tellers
dressed in graffiti's form trailing truth
through multi toned tears, tagged
onto the tapestry of concrete
stapled to yesterday
today and tomorrow.

Like
right now
in a secret garden
guarded by green angels
there is an ancient fruit bearing tree
holding the oldest love letter
carved in its bark
enclosed in
its heart
reading;

Adam 'n' Eve 4 eva

Born
on the same day
as infinity, these are part of the endless
mysteries that litter our daily lives

and if you haven't seen them
yet, someday, you will see them too.

In the citadel of a second
2 nano-moments from now
eleventeen blinks from the next *whenever*
a benevolent eloquent elephant
tipsy on musk, will bow to deer pressure
and donate his tusks to charity.

A leprechaun lost
in solid gold raking
will start gold-baking begonia battered
broomsticks to sweep every residence

where poetry be president
and every man listening
will start clapping,
and the minute after that,
nothing will have happened.

See…
the next minute is as much a mystery
as the mystery that dwells within the *minute*
and that *minute* minute of mystery stretches
far.

It covers empty envelopes marked "top secret".
It is laughter wafting after the day goes down.
It is a poet extracting Iranian juice from a memory
and posing, metaphysically, a prose with its juice.
It is a shadow cut loose.

It is how wind flows through water
awakening wonder in the womb of seeds
vibrating to trees, off springing clouds
that wring water back to wind which whistles
where ever the weather goes…

It is a barefooted, newly born
Nubian, new-being bohemian
in an urban basement, baby-bashing
beats on an upturned wooden basin,
bearing a rhythm older than his own father's
wisdom and not knowing where it came from
just ad-libbing to it in baby speech form.

These mysteries line our streets
and in their midst, I sit
on a mountain top
with my Iranian scented ink
trace words on winds
sink to blue worlds
drink nectar
and think…

   and
     think.

Lightning Source UK Ltd.
Milton Keynes UK
UKHW011320151020
371635UK00003B/1119